11/20/96

D0627769

Courtney's First Cruise

By
Janice Lynne

This book is dedicated to Courtney,
my beautiful lovebird. Courtney's incredible
spirit and loving nature inspired me to write this
book. Thank you, Courtney, for teaching me that
with the power of love, anything is possible.

Hi! My name is Courtney.
Today I'm going with Mommy on a cruise.
Only Mommy doesn't know it yet!
We are packing our bags while singing a tune.
We always sing our special tune when we are happy.

Mommy kisses me goodbye and turns to leave.
This is my big chance!

I jump on Mommy's hat and off we go!
Only Mommy doesn't know it yet!

Here we are at our cruiseship!
It sure is BIG!

As we enter the ship, we have our picture taken.
Then we walk into a big lobby on the ship.

We find our cabin and Mommy opens the door.
Oh no! Mommy is walking to the mirror!

Mommy screams "Ahhhhhh!!" when she sees me.
"Courtney, what are you doing here?"
Then Mommy falls back on the bed.

Oh oh...I think I'm in BIG trouble.
I may be in the biggest trouble I've ever been in!
I'm getting scared.
What if Mommy takes me home?
I better think of something fast!

I know...I show Mommy my suitcase filled with birdseed. Mommy is amazed!
She says "Okay Courtney, you can stay with me on the cruise, just this once."
I hope it won't be just this once.
Only Mommy doesn't know it yet!

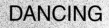

DANCING

VIDEO GAMES

Now that Mommy knows I'm on the ship, she takes me everywhere.

BINGO

SING-A-LONGS

There are so many things to do on a ship.
I am having the best time of my life!

At night, Mommy and I see wonderful shows.

During the day, Mommy and I take a nap on deck.

Sometimes Mommy takes me off the ship
to a beautiful island. Mommy likes to shop
while I make friends with the local birds.

Later, we cool off with a swim in the ocean.
I hope the fish are friendly!
Mommy and I are always happy to return to our ship.

Mommy and I eat our meals in different places on the ship. Sometimes we eat in the dining room.

Other times we order a snack in our cabin and watch a movie.

My favorite place to eat is the buffet with the salad bar. I like it best because it has a big bowl of sunflower seeds. I love sunflower seeds!

I can't stop myself any longer.
I dive off Mommy's hat into the sunflower seeds!

I eat and eat and eat.
I eat until I can't move.
I think I have a tummyache.
I want my Mommy!
Only Mommy doesn't know I'm here!

Oh oh, some children see me and pick me up!
The little girl with pigtails says "That's the bird on the
lady's hat. I heard the lady call the bird 'Courtney'."
They decide to take me to the children's playroom.
Only Mommy doesn't know it yet!

I'm having a great time with the children!
We read books and play lots of games.
Everyone takes turns playing with me!

We even get to paint pictures.
Everyone paints pictures of me!

At dinnertime, the parents come to pick up the children.
They say "Bye bye Courtney, see you after dinner."

All of a sudden, I am all alone.
Mommy didn't pick me up for dinner.
Mommy doesn't know I'm here!
I'm getting scared.
Will Mommy ever find me?
What should I do?

Maybe I should look for Mommy.
I'll never find her on this BIG ship!
Anyway, Mommy said if I should ever get lost,
I should stay in one place.
That way, she can find me.

Maybe she will hear me if I sing our special tune.........
Is that Mommy I hear singing?!

All of a sudden, there she is!
Mommy found me!
This is the happiest moment of my life!

Mommy says "Courtney, I've been looking all over for you! If I hadn't run into the children just now, I may have never found you! Don't ever leave me again!" I've learned my lesson! I will never leave Mommy again! *Only Mommy doesn't know it yet!*

Today is the last day of the cruise.
Mommy and I are packing our bags.
But this time we are not singing.
That's because we are sad to leave our ship.

On our way off the ship, we stop by the photo gallery.
Mommy laughs when she sees our picture.
Then she buys it.

I think I will go with Mommy on all her vacations
Only Mommy doesn't know it yet!

To order additional copies of "Courtney's First Cruise",
fill out this form and send $5.95 plus $1.50 postage &
handling for each book to:

Courtney™ Club
9715 W. Broward Blvd.
Suite 110
Ft. Lauderdale, FL 33324

Courtney™

Name _____

Address _____

City _____

State/Zip_____

Enclosed is my: Check ❏   Money Order ❏

Book Total $_____

Postage & Handling $_____

Applicable Sales Tax $_____
(Florida only)

Total Amount Due $_____

Payable in U.S. funds. No cash orders accepted.

Please allow 4 weeks for delivery.

Where was book purchased? _____

_____